Trouble for Breakfast

SANDY GULLIKSON

Dial Books for Young Readers
New York

For my family

S.G.

Published by Dial Books for Young Readers
A Division of Penguin Books USA Inc.
375 Hudson Street, New York, New York 10014

Design by Nancy R. Leo
Printed in Hong Kong by
South China Printing Company (1988) Limited
W
First Edition
1 3 5 7 9 10 8 6 4 2

Library of Congress Cataloging in Publication Data
Gullikson, Sandy.
Trouble for breakfast / by Sandy Gullikson.
p.   cm.
Summary: When Mrs. C.E. Rabbit gets sick, her children
and their friends try to make her a get-well breakfast
with near-disastrous, but very effective results.
ISBN 0-8037-0775-4.—ISBN 0-8037-0776-2 (lib. bdg.)
[1. Breakfasts—Fiction. 2. Cookery—Fiction.
3. Sick—Fiction. 4. Animals—Fiction.]
I. Title.
PZ7.G9485Tr 1990   [E]—dc20   89-38539   CIP   AC

The art for each picture was created using pen and ink and watercolor.
It was then color-separated and reproduced in full color.

One fine, sunny morning, Rufus and Greyer Coyote came over to visit the Cactus-Eared Rabbits.

It was still early and Munchit and Crunchit, Mrs. C.E. Rabbit's twins, were the only ones up.

"Cousin Arnold the Armadillo is visiting from Somewhere Very Far Away and
he loves to eat bugs!" announced Crunchit excitedly.

"I'm hungry," said Arnold with a yawn. "Is breakfast ready?"

But Mrs. C.E. Rabbit was still in bed.

The group marched to Mrs. C.E.'s door.

At the count of three (Greyer did the counting) they all yelled, "ARE YOU AWAKE?" There was no answer, but for a small movement under the quilt. Greyer could see the rabbit's spikey ears twitching.

"Ohh-arghh-harumph," was all she heard.

Greyer was a little scared. What was wrong?

"Oh! Id's you, Greyer. I thing I hab a code ad a feber ad a sore throde. I'b sig!"
rasped a scratchy-voiced Mrs. C.E. Then she smiled at Greyer weakly.

Everyone was so relieved they all started talking at once.

"Don't worry, Mrs. C.E.," said Greyer, "I'll make the coffee."

"Don't worry, Mrs. C.E.," said Rufus, "I'll make the muffins."

"Don't worry, Mama," chimed in Munchit and Crunchit, "we'll help, we'll help!"

Everything was okay. Greyer, being the oldest, and feeling unusually crabby, hungry, and bossy, took charge. Everyone got a job. Greyer snapped the coffee pot on, then strode to the sink to wash the dishes.

Rufus turned the stove to BAKE and carefully lined up the ingredients for the muffins. Munchit suggested they add some other things like peppermint drops, walnuts, chocolate syrup, some saltines, and a big dollop of peanut butter.

"Mrs. C.E. always fixes chicken soup when we are sick," Greyer announced. All nodded, impressed with her wisdom. She opened a can of soup, plopped it in a saucepan, and added a can of water.

"There," she said, "I'm done." And she sat down to read her magazine.

Munchit and Crunchit dumped the leftover ingredients into the bowl.
This breakfast was going to be perfect!

"I love batter," Arnold said happily, licking sticky driblets from his chin.
Then he started mixing in earnest.

It was all going so smoothly. Rufus went into Mrs. C.E.'s room to bring her a glass of juice. Just then a huge crash sounded from the kitchen. The extra bowl of batter had fallen on the floor with just about everything else!

Greyer swooped down to clean up the eggs and saw Munchit and Crunchit eating gobs of batter.

"*No, no, no, no!*" she cried.

"*Oh, the s-i-i-i-n-k, the s-i-i-i-n-k!*" squealed Arnold.

"Wud's rog?" Mrs. C.E. called.

"Everything's really okay," Arnold told her. But in the kitchen water was running everywhere, and no one wanted to clean it up.

It was Munchit who noticed the oven.

"The muffins are burning!" he shrieked. Greyer reached up, turned off the oven, and bravely pulled them out. They were black and horrible looking. Even Arnold, who would eat just about anything, shouted, "Yuck!"

When the smoke cleared they saw with dismay that the chicken soup and coffee had almost boiled away. Rufus angrily snapped off the burners.

The breakfast was ruined! They all sat down in a sad little huddle in the middle of it all.

Rufus picked up one of the muffins and dropped it in disgust. It sounded like a stone when it hit. *Bink!* An idea popped into his head.

"We could build a house of muffins! We could stick the muffins together with butter!"

"Butter! Yum!" Arnold agreed, licking his lips.

"Just like a gingerbread house," joined in Greyer, who wished she had thought of such a clever idea first.

Munchit and Crunchit found a tray.

And they all worked on the muffin house together.

Greyer went over to the stove and peered into the soup pan.

"Why, there's just enough soup to fill a bowl!" she exclaimed. "Now Mrs. C.E. will surely get better." The coffee is okay too, she thought, as she poured it thick and black into Mrs. C.E.'s favorite cup. Just needs a little sugar. Then she carefully placed both into the little muffin house.

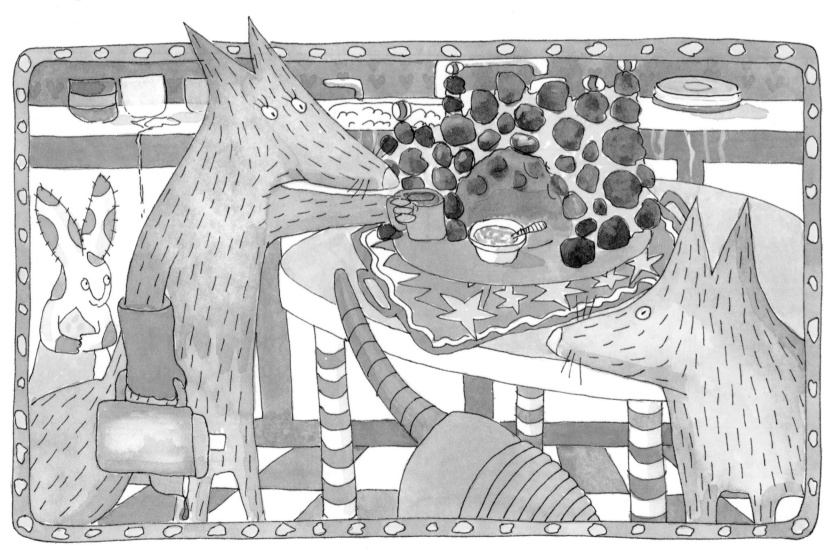

Finally it was done! Arnold, who was the strongest, led the way, carrying the tray in to Mrs. C.E., who had been waiting and wondering, as you might imagine.

"Look at our muffin house!" cried out Crunchit. "I scraped the batter off the floor!"

"And I put it back in the pan," said Munchit. Greyer glared at them and showed Mrs. C.E. how the little door worked.

Mrs. C.E. carefully pulled out the small sticky cup and the bowl of soup. She sipped the coffee. "How excellend," she said. They all smiled at each other with relief and happiness. When she tasted the soup and smacked her lips appreciatively they jumped up and down and made little squeaks.

"Oh, I thing I'b gedding bedder. I thing I'll ged ub," Mama said. She hopped out of bed and headed straight for the kitchen.

In a panic, Greyer, Arnold, Munchit, Crunchit, and Rufus raced by her down the hall.

What if . . . oh, no! . . . she . . . sees . . . our . . . mess . . . oh, no! Their thoughts tumbled over and over as they ran.

Rufus was last, and just as Mrs. C.E. reached the kitchen he turned to her and yelled,

"DON'T WORRY . . . EVERYTHING'S OKAY!"

And so it was.